# ROBOTICS

## Tony Potter and Ivor Guild

### Designed by Roger Priddy

With thanks to Nigel Prue
(The National Advanced Robotics Research Centre)
and Michael Skidmore

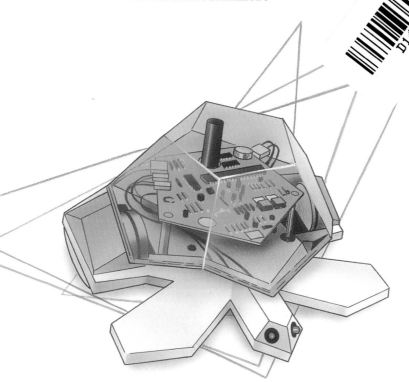

## Consultant Editor: Nigel East
## Editor: Lynn Myring

Illustrated by: Jeremy Gower, Chris Lyon, Simon Roulstone,
Martin Newton, Geoff Dicks, Mick Gillah, Rob McCaig,
Tim Cowdell, Janos Mariffy, Mike Saunders,
Kuo Kang Chen, Stan North, Guy Smith.

With additional designs by John Russell

# CONTENTS

# About robotics

The word "robot" comes from the Czech word *robota*, meaning "slave-like work". It was first introduced in the 1920s by the writer, Karel Čapek* in *Rossum's Universal Robots*. Invented by the imaginary scientist, Rossum, the robots in this play were simply intended to help humans by performing basic, repetitive tasks. However, when the robots are eventually used to fight in war, the play takes a tragic turn. The robots revolt, kill their human owners and finally take over the world.

There are many robots in existence today, but they are quite different from the robots of science fiction films and books. Instead of being frightening, super-intelligent metal people, real robots are just machines that are controlled by a computer

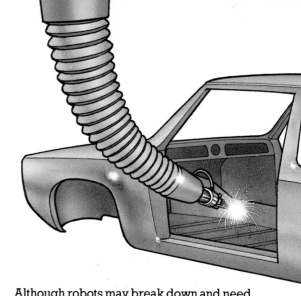

Although robots may break down and need routine servicing like cars, they never need holidays, sleep or meal breaks.

Many factories prefer to use robots rather than other automatic machines

to work in a set way. They have difficulty in moving around and have no intelligence of their own. Early robots were unable to "see" and had no basic sense of taste, smell, touch or hearing. However, advances in technology mean that robots are now being made with sensors – a TV camera "eye" or a microphone "ear" for instance – which give them limited electronic senses of sight and hearing. It is also possible to equip today's advanced robots with touch sensors and even to add some logic facilities and intelligence to their computer control systems.

Robots are used to do many things, often jobs which are very dangerous or tiring for people, such as welding car bodies. In factories, robots carry out repetitive tasks without getting tired and in some cases their accuracy enables them to perform tasks more efficiently than people.

because they can be programmed to do different jobs. Also, a new program can be stored in the computer for when a job needs to be done again in weeks, months or even years, without the need for reteaching or learning a job again.

Some robots are used to do jobs that would be impossible for people to do, such as working inside the radioactive part of a nuclear power station, or visiting distant planets. Others, like the small micro-robots used with a home computer, are for learning about robotics or just for fun.

3

*Pronounced Chapek*

# What robots can and cannot do

Robots are able to do many different tasks, especially in factories. Here they are carefully maintained and organized to work alongside other automatic machines. Robots are rarely set up to work outside the factory because it is much more difficult to get them to work away from a carefully ordered environment.

Science fiction robots are often made to look human, but the appearance and ability of an industrial robot depend on the kind of work it has to do. Because they only need to work from a single position, the majority of industrial robots are either bolted to the floor or to an overhead frame, called a gantry. They look like "arms" and are often called manipulative robots because they hold things, like the welding torch below.

Robot arms are most familiar in car factories, but they can be found in many other industries – electronics, engineering, clothing and confectionery factories, for example. The jobs they are best at are those that involve doing the same thing over and over again.

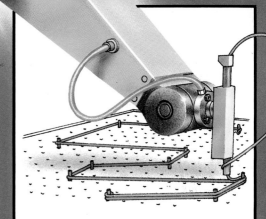

## Accurate robots

Some robots are able to do very accurate and intricate work, but this depends on the design of the robot and the computer program that controls it. This picture shows a robot laying out lengths of wire in a complex pattern for wiring-up electric vehicles, like fork-lift trucks. To do this, it first has to push nails into holes in a pegboard according to a pattern stored in its computer memory. The robot has to line up the nails with the holes very precisely to get them to fit.

## Robots today

Most robots are only able to work in a factory where everything is carefully organized around them. For example, robots are usually next to a conveyor belt which "feeds" them with work, and most are kept in a wire "cage" to prevent them from injuring people nearby. In some advanced factories robots are guarded by an invisible curtain of infra-red light or a surveillance camera. Both of these stop the robot from working while people are in the danger area.

Some scientists are already working with robots that will be capable of working anywhere. These are extremely "intelligent". They have sensors which enable them to react to a vast amount of information (feedback) from their surroundings. However, most advanced robots still cannot react fast enough to catch a ball, for instance. Imagine trying to do this with thick mittens on, one hand tied behind your back, your eyes blindfolded, feet cemented to the ground and your ears covered. Most robots have to work with these limitations.

## Tough robots

Many robots can do work that would be dangerous or unpleasant for people. Robots are generally quite strong because they are made of metal, and can withstand extreme conditions, such as a hot, poisonous atmosphere. This robot is putting its hand into a red-hot oven to take a metal casting out. The heat does not affect its performance, so it is able to produce high quality castings by always taking them out at exactly the right temperature.

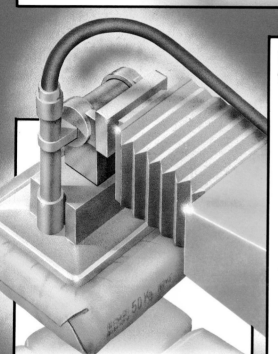

## How strong is a robot?

The strength of a robot depends on the power of its motors and the task it was designed for. For example, a home micro-robot, made from thin sheet metal, can only lift the weight of an apple; a large industrial robot, like the one above, could pick up something as heavy as a whole car body in a single movement. A robot like this can easily lift all day, whereas even if a strong person could lift a car, they would soon get tired and start to slow down.

## What happens when things go wrong?

Robots without sensors are unable to react to anything unexpected happening to them. The computer-controlled robot, pictured below, sprays bicycle frames as they pass along a conveyor belt. If a frame falls off, the robot continues spraying. One way of preventing this is to put a switch on the conveyor that is linked to the computer. This turns the robot off until another bicycle frame is detected within the robot's reach.

This robot wears a plastic cover as an "overall" to stop paint from clogging it up. Other robots, such as those used for cleaning parts of a furnace, also need special covers.

# Mobile robots

A mobile robot is a computer-controlled vehicle, and the most common have wheels or tracks. Some carry a computer around with them, but others are connected to a computer by a long cable or a radio link. Robot vehicles are used in many factories to move goods and materials around, sometimes from one fixed robot arm to another. They move around the factory by following white lines on the floor, or magnetic signals from cables buried underground. The robot's computer is programmed to tell it which lines or cables to follow. Advanced mobile robots can have a map stored in their computer control systems. With the use of sensors, this enables the vehicle to steer a safe path between different work stations.

## How robots follow buried cables

## Steering a robot

This is a mobile micro-robot. It is steered by two motors driving the central wheels. Its computer controls the steering by changing the speed and direction of the motors. The robot's other wheels just prevent it from tipping up.

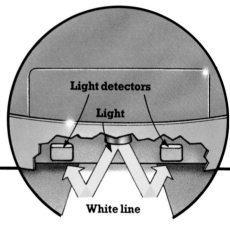

Light detectors

Light

White line

## How robots follow lines

The circle above shows how a robot can follow lines by using a sensor to send feedback to the computer about its position over the line. The sensor usually consists of a light pointing to the floor with a light detector picking up the reflections from either side of it. If the robot starts to move off the line, a message is sent to the computer to correct the steering.

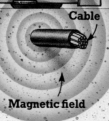

Bumper    Sensor

Cable

Magnetic field

A cable-following robot like the one above usually has two coils of wire fixed to the front, which are used as sensors to detect the magnetic field surrounding an underground cable. The magnetic field is made by sending electricity through the cable, which creates a small electric current in the robot's sensors. The strength of the current in the sensors alters according to how far the robot is from the cable. The computer steers the robot over the cable by balancing the strength of current in the two sensor coils.

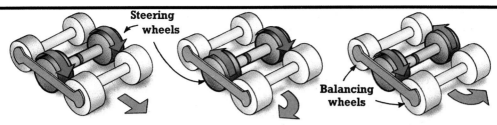

**Forward or backward:** Both wheels are driven at the same speed and in the same direction.

**Right turn:** The left-hand wheel is driven forward, and the right-hand wheel backward.

**Left turn:** The right-hand wheel is driven forward, and the left-hand wheel backward.

Robots with tracks can also be steered like this because each track is like a driven wheel.

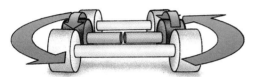

This kind of robot steers by turning on the spot. Robots can also be steered gradually as they move forward by making both motors go forward, with one going faster.

**Steering mechanism**

Some robots use a steering mechanism like that of a car. However, instead of a steering wheel they have a motor connected to a computer. Robots like this are less mobile because they cannot turn on the spot.

## Roving robot

Some mobile robots do not need guides, like white lines. Instead, an on-board computer does the navigating. Robots of this type are used for dangerous tasks, such as carrying out repairs in nuclear power stations or searching buildings for bombs or gas leaks.

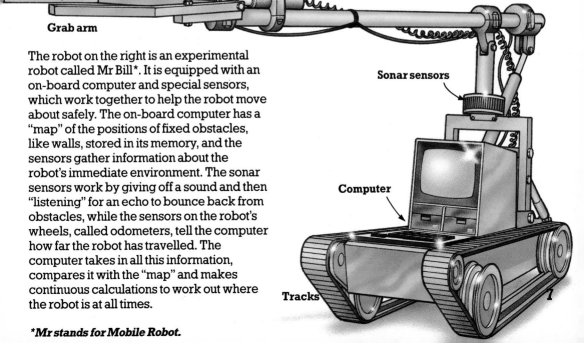

**Grab arm**

The robot on the right is an experimental robot called Mr Bill*. It is equipped with an on-board computer and special sensors, which work together to help the robot move about safely. The on-board computer has a "map" of the positions of fixed obstacles, like walls, stored in its memory, and the sensors gather information about the robot's immediate environment. The sonar sensors work by giving off a sound and then "listening" for an echo to bounce back from obstacles, while the sensors on the robot's wheels, called odometers, tell the computer how far the robot has travelled. The computer takes in all this information, compares it with the "map" and makes continuous calculations to work out where the robot is at all times.

**Sonar sensors**

**Computer**

**Tracks**

*Mr stands for Mobile Robot.*

# How robot arms work

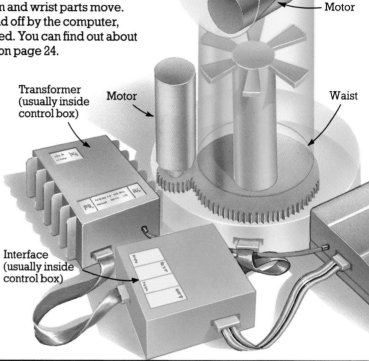

There are many different ways of constructing and powering a robot. These pages show all the things that are needed to make a robot arm work, together with a view of the inside of the robot showing what makes it move. Some industrial robots work in a similar way, but their construction is much more complicated.

A robot arm is jointed like a human arm and is driven by electric motors. Each moving part is usually driven by a separate source of power. The one shown here has six motors to make its arm and wrist parts move. Each motor is switched on and off by the computer, which also controls their speed. You can find out about other ways of driving robots on page 24.

Shoulder

Gear

Motor

Waist

## Control box

The control box contains both the transformer and the interface (shown here outside the box). Electricity for the robot's motors and computer is provided by the transformer. This converts the high electric voltage from the mains into a low voltage for the computer. The interface links the transformer, motors and computer together. Inside is an electronic circuit which switches the power to the motors on and off when instructed by the computer.

Transformer (usually inside control box)

Motor

Interface (usually inside control box)

## Arm movements

**Waist** (side to side)

**Shoulder** (up and down)

**Elbow** (in and out)

Most robot arms have three main parts which are joined together. The point where one part is fixed to another is usually called a joint or axis. The joints on a robot, like the one above, are given the names elbow, shoulder and waist. Each axis gives the robot one "degree of freedom" because it allows the parts fixed at the joint to move in a certain way. In these pictures you can see the direction in which each joint allows the robot to move.

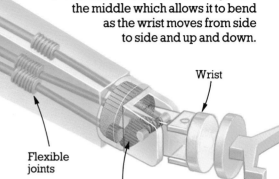

There are three small motors inside the robot's "forearm" which drive three moving parts in the wrist. These motors are connected to gears in the wrist by long shafts. Each shaft has a flexible joint in the middle which allows it to bend as the wrist moves from side to side and up and down.

Elbow

Motors

Wrist

Each motor is connected by gears to a shaft which moves part of the robot. In this picture the shafts are the parts painted orange, and the gears are painted green. The gears help to control the speed of the motors.

Flexible joints

Gears

Gripper

Programming panel

The computer is programmed using the keyboard. It controls everything the robot does by sending a sequence of instructions to the interface. Many robots use a hand-held keyboard like a calculator.

The wrist is a complicated mechanism which can bend in three ways, as shown in the picture below. Some robots have wrists which bend in only two directions, but this is sufficient for the type of work they have to do. The more joints in the wrist, the more capable the robot is to make fine movements to do a job. The robot's hand, called a gripper, is shown separated from its wrist in this picture. You can find out how grippers work on page 26.

# Wrist movements

**Roll** (twist)   **Pitch** (up and down)    **Yaw** (side to side)

Between the gripper and the end of the robot arm is a kind of wrist. Like the arm, the wrist usually has three joints, or axes of rotation. These allow the gripper to move in three ways, shown in the pictures above. These movements have special names: yaw, pitch and roll. A robot like this which can make six kinds of movements has six degrees of freedom. Some robots have more than this, some less, depending on the kind of work they do.

# Designing robots

It is very difficult to design and build a robot, even to do a simple job. A robot designer has to begin by breaking down the job into as many steps as possible to see what sort of robot is needed. For example, without the ability to bend its wrist, the robot arm below spills a glass of water when it lifts it. These pages show an imaginary robot servant designed to do all the dusting around the house. An extremely complex robot is needed to do this apparently simple task. Experts think it may be possible to build a robot like this in a few years' time.

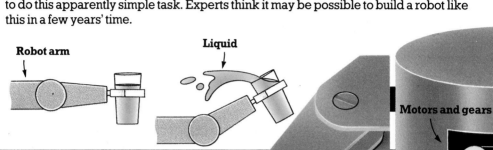

**Robot arm**

**Liquid**

## Computer control

The computer has to be programmed to control everything the robot does: how the motors drive its arms and legs, how it navigates around the house without causing damage, the way it does its dusting, and so on. The computer must make the robot do everything in the right order, such as opening doors before going through them. It also has to work things out without delay so that the robot can respond instantly to something unexpected, like a baby crawling under its feet, or finding that the furniture has been moved.

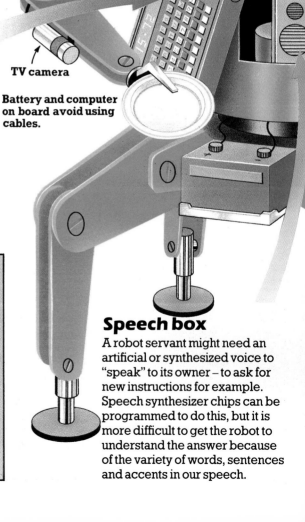

**Motors and gears**

**TV camera**

**Battery and computer on board avoid using cables.**

## The program

An extremely complex program would be needed for the computer because the robot's job involves hundreds of choices based on information, or data, about the world around it. This part of the design, called the software, gives the robot "intelligence" so that it can "decide" what to do.

## Speech box

A robot servant might need an artificial or synthesized voice to "speak" to its owner – to ask for new instructions for example. Speech synthesizer chips can be programmed to do this, but it is more difficult to get the robot to understand the answer because of the variety of words, sentences and accents in our speech.

## Arms

The robot has two arms because it needs to be able to hold objects while dusting underneath. Fixed to one arm it could also have a spray-can of polish, with a computer-controlled plunger to release the polish. This would avoid the need for a third arm to hold the can.

### Design your own robot

Try designing a robot to do one of these jobs:
1 Take a dog for a walk
2 Wash the dishes
3 Mow the lawn

## Sensors

Different kinds of sensors are required for the robot to do its job: navigation sensors for the robot to find its way around, TV camera "eyes" so that it can "see" what it is doing, and safety touch sensors which stop it if it accidentally bumps into anything. All the data from the sensors is sent to the computer via an interface so that it can control the robot's actions.

**Pressurized can of polish**

## Legs

This robot needs at least four legs to climb the steep stairs of a house – something it could not do with wheels or tracks. A Japanese designer has actually built a four-legged, stair-climbing robot.

## Walking robots

It is difficult for a robot to move around on fewer than four legs. Here are some of the problems:

### One leg

A one-legged robot like this has to keep hopping to balance, so it would not be much good for a job like dusting.

### Two legs

When a two-legged robot takes one foot off the ground to walk, it has to balance on the other foot. This is very difficult for the computer to control.

### Three legs

A three-legged robot is very stable standing still, but as soon as it takes one foot off the ground to walk it falls over.

### Four legs

A four-legged robot walks by moving one leg at a time. This means it always has three legs on the ground to balance with.

11

# Special purpose robots

These pages show robots that have been specially designed to do particular jobs.
Industrial robots can often be adapted for different tasks, but some jobs may need a
completely new kind of design.

## Sheep shearer

This is an experimental
robot, designed to shear
sheep while holding them
in a cradle with straps.
The special electric
clippers are fitted with
sonar or ultrasonic
sensors*, which produce
a "map" of the sheep's
shape for the robot's
computer. This "map",
together with continual
feedback from the sensors,
enables the robot to
position the clippers just
above the sheep's skin.
If the sheep wriggles, the
robot can react in less than
one ten-thousandth of a
second to move the
clippers away.

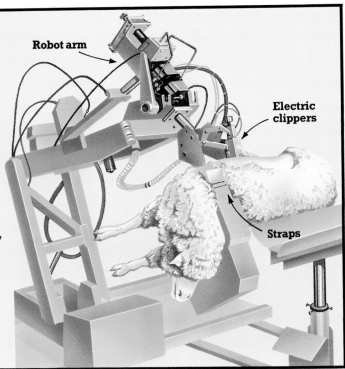

**Robot arm**

**Electric clippers**

**Straps**

## Robot patient

This robot patient is designed to respond
to treatment by students and can even
"die" if someone makes a mistake.
Computer-controlled electronic
components inside the robot can be
programmed to imitate breathing,
heartbeat and blood pressure. Sensors
inside the body measure the efficiency
of a student's treatment.

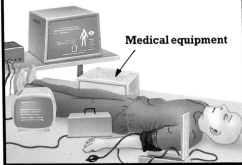

**Medical equipment**

## Robot hand

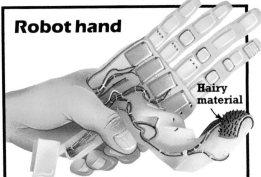

**Hairy material**

The picture above shows an
experimental microchip-controlled
false hand, which is activated by
muscles in the wearer's arm. There is a
microphone in the thumb covered by a
strip of hairy material. The microphone
"listens" for the rustling sound the
material makes when an object is held.
As the hairs are crushed, the sound
stops, which tells the computer the grip
is tight enough.

*See page 32

## Walking robot

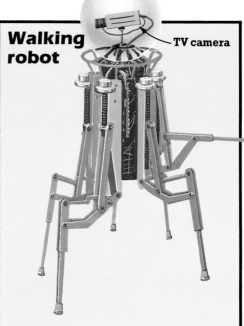

TV camera

## Robot diver

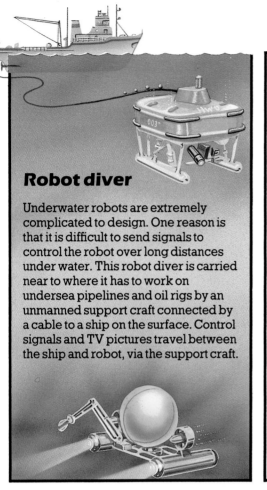

Underwater robots are extremely complicated to design. One reason is that it is difficult to send signals to control the robot over long distances under water. This robot diver is carried near to where it has to work on undersea pipelines and oil rigs by an unmanned support craft connected by a cable to a ship on the surface. Control signals and TV pictures travel between the ship and robot, via the support craft.

This robot is able to walk over rough ground and go up stairs by adjusting the length of its legs. Inside the plastic dome at the top is a TV camera which sends pictures to a computer in the middle of the robot. The robot can walk around outside using solar power to keep its batteries charged.

## Free-roving robotics teacher

Hero 1 is a robot designed to help people at school or in industry learn about robotics. It is a combined mobile and arm robot with lots of different sensors, so that students can discover what robots are and how they work. The robot has a voice synthesizer which can be programmed via its built-in computer, and also sensors to avoid collisions with students and obstacles.

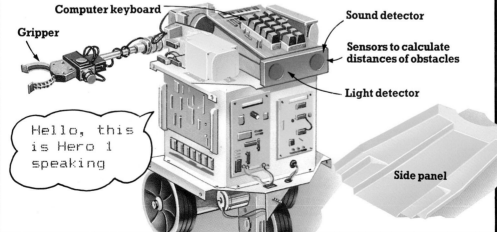

Computer keyboard

Gripper

Sound detector

Sensors to calculate distances of obstacles

Light detector

Hello, this is Hero 1 speaking

Side panel

# Robots in space

Robots are particularly useful for doing jobs in space because it is such a hostile environment for humans to work in. In the future, robots and other automatic machines may make up most of the space workforce.

## Space robot arm

The Space Shuttle can be fitted with a long, folding robot arm as part of its equipment. This is used for launching satellites and other machines from its cargo hold, or retrieving them from space for repair. The arm folds neatly out of the way in the cargo hold after use.

Cargo

Shoulder joint

Cargo hold

TV camera

Elbow joint

Shiny blanket

The arm, called RMS (Remote Manipulator System), has its own computer which is programmed to make different sets of movements. It can also be controlled from the flight deck with joysticks similar to those used with computer games. Up to eight cameras can be positioned on the arm so that the operator can see what to do.

The RMS is capable of lifting an object which would weigh about the same as fifteen cars on Earth. It is designed to cope with twice as much in an emergency. If the arm gets stuck and prevents the cargo doors from closing it can be jettisoned into space.

A shiny blanket covers the whole arm so that it reflects the Sun's heat and does not get too hot. There are also heating elements inside the blanket to keep the arm warm when the Shuttle is on the night side of Earth.

Each joint is driven by a tiny electric motor. Sensors on the joints tell the computer the position of the arm.

TV camera

Wrist joint

## Satellites

Satellites often include components like sensors and computers, but are really automatic machines rather than robots. The sensors on satellites are often used to collect data rather than to provide feedback for its computer.

**Stretched out, the arm can reach nearly as far as the length of two buses put together.**

14

## Robot missiles

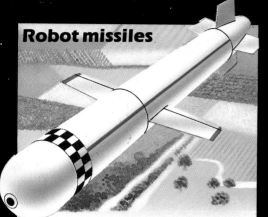

Some kinds of missiles are described by experts as robots. They are programmed to reach a target automatically using sensors and an on-board computer. Cruise missiles, for example, use sensors to "see" the ground below, and then compare this data with a computerized route map. This enables them to fly very low to avoid radar detection.

## Space probes

Soil analysis equipment

Weather equipment

Soil-collecting scoop

Apart from the moon, exploration of other planets and moons in the solar system has been made only by robot spacecraft. This is mainly because of the time it takes to reach them – Voyager 1 took 18 months to reach Jupiter, for example. This picture shows a computer-controlled robot landing-craft sent to the surface of Mars by Viking 1.

## How the arm picks things up

The end of the arm has a special gripping and latching mechanism which can be remotely operated to hold satellites and other cargo. Each piece of cargo has a shaft sticking out of one end. The end of the arm is manipulated over the shaft, and then rotated. This twists the locking unit onto the tapered shaft so that the cargo is pulled tightly against the end of the arm. The end of the arm is simply rotated in the opposite direction to release the shaft.

The picture below shows the arm releasing a telecommunications satellite into orbit above the Earth.

Solar panels

Shaft

End gripper

15

# Micro-robots

A micro-robot is a small, educational robot controlled by a home computer. You can find out about three different micro-robots on these pages.

## Buggy

The robot on the right is made from a LEGO Dacta Technic construction kit. It can be operated using either a battery and manual controls or through a computer.

An optosensor on the front of the buggy enables the robot to "see" whatever it is travelling over. It transmits an invisible infra-red light onto the ground below, which then reflects light back to the sensor. The computer can use the data from the optosensor to "see" a line like the one in the picture and tell the robot to follow it, or "read" a bar code. It can also be programmed to translate the bar code into musical notes so that the buggy plays a tune as it moves around on the floor.

If equipped with touch sensors and bumpers, the robot will even reverse automatically if it hits something.

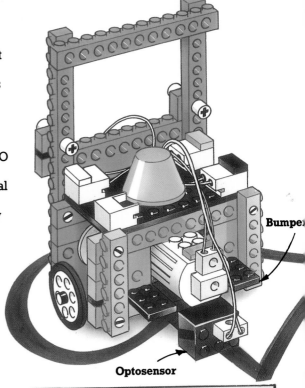

**Bumper**

**Optosensor**

## How to connect up a micro-robot

These pictures show how a micro-robot arm is connected to a home computer and to a power supply.

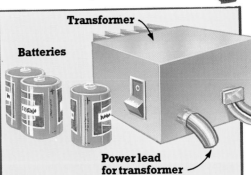

**Transformer**

**Batteries**

**Power lead for transformer**

Most micro-robots are driven by low voltage electric motors, so a transformer or batteries are used to power them. This power supply is usually connected to an electronic interface.

**Port**

**It is very dangerous to plug a micro-robot into mains electricity.**

Wires, known as control lines, which control the robot's motors, are plugged into a socket in the computer, called a port. (Not all home computers have the right ports to be able to do this.) One wire is often used for each motor.

## Armdroid

The micro-robot arm shown on the right is called Armdroid. It is used for learning about robotics, or for doing very light work.

Gears to move arm

Motors

The interface is connected to the robot's motors. It is made of electronic components which switch the power to the motors on and off when the computer sends signals to them. Sometimes this circuit is in a separate box, but it can be inside the robot or the computer.

## Drawing robot

The Turtle is a mobile robot which can be programmed to draw with a pen as it moves around. It is remotely controlled by infra-red signals from a computer via an interface.

The robot follows commands in a computer language called LOGO to draw simple shapes like squares or triangles. LOGO uses commands such as FD 10 for forward 10 units and RT 90 for right 90°. The size of these units can easily be changed by using software packages other than LOGO.

The pen is positioned at the back of the Turtle. It is raised and lowered by a motor using the commands "Penup" and "Pendown". Two special purpose motors drive the wheels. An electronic control board provides all of the infra-red reception, decoding and control abilities the Turtle needs to perform the computer commands accurately.

By programming the computer, the shapes drawn by the Turtle can be combined into pictures.

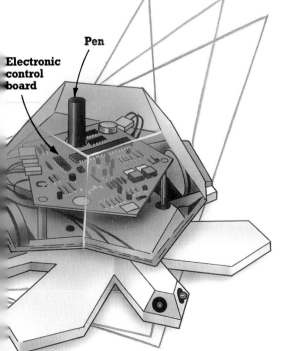

Pen

Electronic control board

# Robot factory workers

Many factories now are almost totally unmanned, with most of the work being carried out by computer-controlled robots. Car plants are among the most highly automated factories in the world. This picture shows how robots and other automatic machines, like conveyor belts and stackers, are used alongside each other to manufacture and assemble parts for cars. People who once used to work on the production line are now employed to carry out routine maintenance or to program the computers.

## Welding station

The framework over the conveyor, shown on the right, is a welding station. Car body panels, lightly tacked together elsewhere in the factory, are welded by six robots into tough, rigid car bodies, as they pass beneath. A glass partition protects the paint area from dangerous sparks. These six robots, working together, assemble cars at a rate of 50 or more per hour.

## Machining centre

The robots below are part of a system called a machining centre, or cell. Heavy lumps of steel enter this area on an automatic shuttle, which is like a tiny flat truck on wheels. The truck carries the steel on a pallet – a wooden or metal tray used to stack materials for transport. One robot is programmed to unload the raw steel from the pallet. The steel is then ready for the "serving" robot, which loads it into the lathes.

Computers in metal cabinets

Welding station

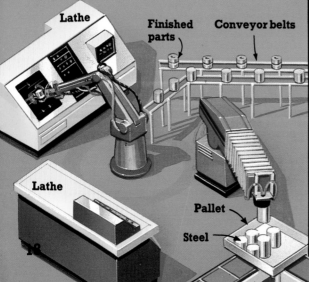

Lathe

Finished parts

Conveyor belts

Lathe

Pallet

Steel

The lathes can be programmed to make many different parts – for axles, gearboxes, engines and so on. The "serving" robot then unloads the finished parts onto the moving conveyor belts for assembly or finishing in another part of the factory.

One computer is in charge of all the computer-controlled robots, lathes and conveyors. This makes sure each machine does the right thing at the right time, to avoid collisions and damage.

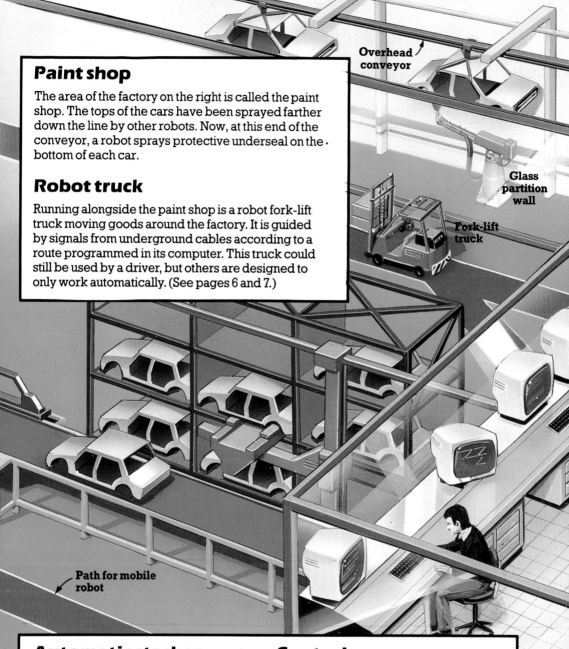

## Paint shop

The area of the factory on the right is called the paint shop. The tops of the cars have been sprayed farther down the line by other robots. Now, at this end of the conveyor, a robot sprays protective underseal on the bottom of each car.

## Robot truck

Running alongside the paint shop is a robot fork-lift truck moving goods around the factory. It is guided by signals from underground cables according to a route programmed in its computer. This truck could still be used by a driver, but others are designed to only work automatically. (See pages 6 and 7.)

**Overhead conveyor**

**Glass partition wall**

**Fork-lift truck**

**Path for mobile robot**

## Automatic stacker

The orange machine above is called an automatic stacker. It is programmed to place partly completed cars in a rack until they are needed. It saves floor space because it stacks things vertically. The same kind of computer-controlled stacker is used in Japanese cities to park bicycles. Some experts say these are robots because they can be programmed to stack different things, but others disagree.

## Control room

Above is the control room where all the automatic operations carried out in the factory are controlled and monitored. It is the computers in here that organize the computer-controlled robots and machines. An operator watches the display screens to check that all the machines are working properly and that production targets are being met. Systems like this are already in use all over the world.

# How to teach a robot

A robot's computer has to be given a set of instructions called a program to get it to work. This is done either by guiding the robot through a sequence of movements, and programming the computer to remember them, or by instructing the computer directly with the keyboard. In this way, the robot can be made to "learn" a set of movements, and repeat them over and over again.

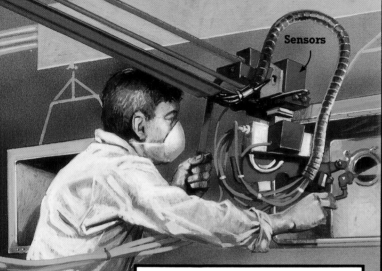

Sensors

## Remote teaching

Robots can be taught remotely with a computer keyboard, or a simplified keyboard called a teach pendant. This is connnected to the computer and has commands like UP, DOWN, LEFT and RIGHT, which can be used to position the robot. The computer memorizes the robot's movements by means of a TEACH button used by the operator.

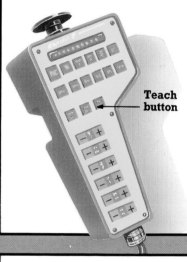

Teach button

## Showing a robot arm what to do

One way of teaching a robot is by guiding its arm through the movements needed to do a job. This is called lead-through programming. The robot in this picture is being taught to spray paint by a person skilled at the job.

First the computer is programmed to remember the movements shown to the robot, and the order they were made in. Then the computer is programmed to make the robot automatically follow the path it was taught. It is very important that the computer repeats this exactly, otherwise the robot would spray paint in the wrong pattern and make a mess. Sensors on the robot's joints send data to the computer about its position. Special safety units are used with this type of robot to ensure it does not start automatically while the man is still holding the spray head.

## Direct control

Forward 10
Left 90
Forward 24
Left 45
Forward 35

This micro-robot is called the Zeaker. It can be programmed to move around, using a computer language with similar commands to LOGO. It can also be used for drawing as there is a pen fixed under its body.

# Talking to robots

Micro-robot arm

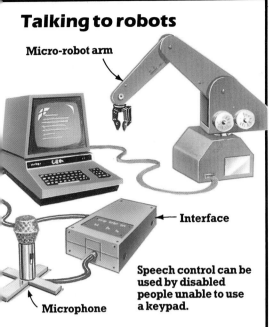

Interface

Microphone

Speech control can be used by disabled people unable to use a keypad.

Spoken instructions, or "direct programming", may soon be used to control robots. Experiments are being carried out where a special interface connects a microphone to the computer and converts spoken commands, such as "up" or "down", into electrical signals. The computer is programmed to recognize these as instructions for the robot.

The program, or software, which comes with the Zeaker lets the user direct its movements by pressing keys on the computer. A sequence of movements can be built up in the computer's memory and repeated over and over again to get the robot to draw complex patterns.

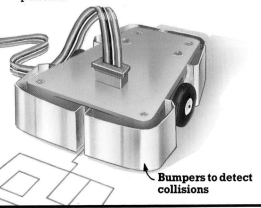

Bumpers to detect collisions

# Chocolate-box packer

For some jobs, like picking things up and putting them down, the robot only needs to know precisely the points to start and finish at. The robot can be shown what to do by being guided to these points, by hand or with a teach pendant, and then getting its computer to remember them. The computer is programmed to work out the route the robot takes between the points. Industrial robots are taught to do loading and simple assembly jobs in this way.

In a factory the box would be on a conveyor.

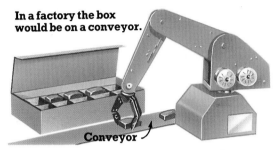

Conveyor

**Step 1:** The robot is guided to the chocolate and its computer is told to remember the position where it has to open and close its gripper.

**Step 2:** The robot is guided to the point where it has to drop the chocolate into the box, and the computer instructed to remember it.

**Step 3:** The stopping and starting points are now in the computer's memory. The computer can instruct the robot to repeat the movement over and over again.

# Types of robot arm

There are several main types of robot arm, each designed to be able to move in different ways according to how its moving parts are put together. The design of a robot is called its architecture, and the space it can move around in as a result of its design is called its working envelope – shaded blue on these pages.

Jointed-arm robot

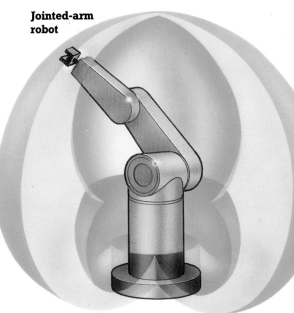

## Jointed-arm robots

The design of a jointed-arm robot is based on the human arm. The one on the right has a rotating base part which is not able to go all the way around. The arm is jointed at the shoulder and elbow and can move like a hinge at both joints. The working envelope of a jointed-arm robot is shaped like part of a ball.

Spherical robot

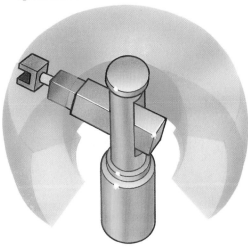

## Spherical or Polar robots

This type of robot gets its name from the spherical working envelope it is able to move in. The main arm part of the robot on the left moves in and out like a telescope, and also has a hinge-like joint at the shoulder. The robot's waist rotates, but it cannot turn 360°. The design of spherical robots makes them very strong, so they are often used to pick up heavy weights – sometimes as much as the weight of a car.

XYZ robot

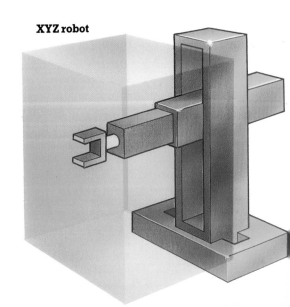

## XYZ robots

Robots like the one on the right get their name because they are able to move in three different directions called X, Y and Z and have a cube-shaped working envelope. The robot's side-to-side movement on its base is called direction X. The main arm part goes in and out telescopically, and this is direction Y. This part of the arm also moves up and down in direction Z. The design of XYZ robots makes them very accurate. so they are often used to do precise jobs, such as

assembly.

# Cylindrical robots

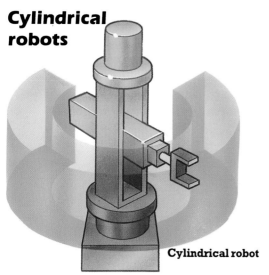

**Cylindrical robot**

The main arm part of a cylindrical robot moves in and out telescopically, and is also fixed to a "pole" at the shoulder so that it can slide up and down. The "pole" rotates, although not all the way around, and this gives the robot a working envelope shaped like a cylinder.

## Spine robot

This type of robot is designed on the same principle as the human spine. The spine robot can reach almost anywhere within its working envelope, even back into the middle, so it can work in inaccessible spaces like the inside of a car. The arm can also swing right around in a circle over and over again.

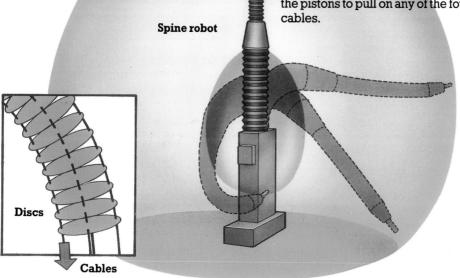

**Spine robot**

**Discs**

**Cables**

## Your working envelope

To calculate the volume of your own working envelope, you will need a friend's help to measure yourself from the floor to the highest point you can reach above your head (H), and from your nose to your outstretched fingers (R). Put these measurements in place of the letters in the formula. Your answer should be in cubic centimetres or cubic inches, depending on which units of measurement you use.

Formula:

$$(3.14 \times R \times R \times H) + (\tfrac{2}{3} \times 3.14 \times R \times R \times R) =$$

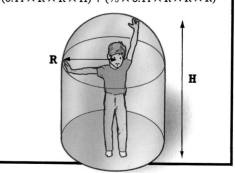

Inside its concertina cover are lots of discs assembled on top of each other. The robot can be made longer or shorter by adding or removing discs. The discs are held together by two pairs of cables which are fixed to pistons in the base. The robot's computer controls the spine by moving the pistons to pull on any of the four cables.

# How robots are driven

Each moving part of a robot is driven separately, either by an electric motor or by a hydraulic or pneumatic system. In order to control the robot to move quickly or slowly, it must be possible to alter the speed of the drive. Mobile robots are usually electrically driven, but the kind of drive used on a robot arm depends on the work it has to do. Hydraulic robots are often used for moving very heavy loads, and electric drive motors are best for robots used to assemble electronic circuits.

## Electric motors

Many different types of electric motor are used to drive robots. One type often used is a direct current, or d.c., motor. You can see below what a simple d.c. motor looks like inside.

At the top are fixed contacts connected to an electrical supply, such as a battery. A wire is coiled around the iron core from top to bottom. When electricity flows through this wire, a magnetic field is produced. This opposes the magnetic field between the North and South poles of the horseshoe magnet. The wire is thrust out of the magnet's more powerful field and makes a half turn.

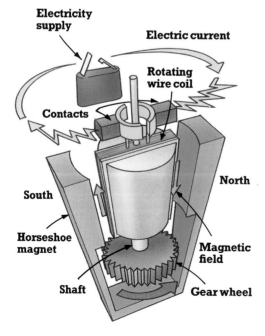

Electricity supply

Electric current

Rotating wire coil

Contacts

South

North

Horseshoe magnet

Shaft

Magnetic field

Gear wheel

## Hydraulic systems

A hydraulic system works like a syringe used for injections. It can be used to make either circular or straight movements according to the construction.

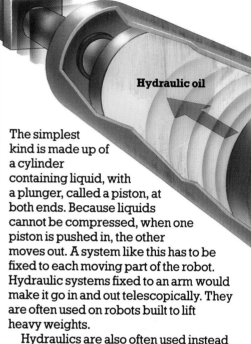

End of robot arm

Hydraulic oil

The simplest kind is made up of a cylinder containing liquid, with a plunger, called a piston, at both ends. Because liquids cannot be compressed, when one piston is pushed in, the other moves out. A system like this has to be fixed to each moving part of the robot. Hydraulic systems fixed to an arm would make it go in and out telescopically. They are often used on robots built to lift heavy weights.

Hydraulics are also often used instead of electric motors where there is a danger of sparks from a motor igniting fumes in the atmosphere of a factory, such as the paint area in a car factory.

The current through the wire is reversed by every half turn, so the magnetic forces are always in opposition and always reject each other. This keeps the coil rotating in the same direction, and turns the shaft. The gear at the bottom of the shaft could be attached to a robot and used to drive it when the motor is switched on.

The speed of a motor like this can be reduced or increased using gears. The speed can also be varied electrically with a device similar to the foot control on an electric sewing machine. The strength of a robot partly depends on the speed of its motors – usually the slower the motor the more power it has.

There are different ways of pushing the pistons in and out on a hydraulic system – the type used on car brakes, for example, is operated by a person pressing the brake pedal. On a robot, however, the piston has to be pushed by some electrically operated device for the computer to be able to control it. This picture shows a device called a solenoid fixed to a shaft on the end of the piston. This too has a piston inside which is pushed in and out by an electromagnet.

## Pneumatic systems

In a pneumatic system, air, or some other gas is used to move a mechanical part of the robot, often the gripper. A simple system consists of a cylinder with a piston inside which is connected to a shaft on the robot. Compressed air is let into one end of the cylinder by a computer-controlled electric valve. The air forces the piston forward, which in turn moves the jaws of the gripper. Pneumatic systems are often used for grippers because gases compress and make the jaws more responsive.

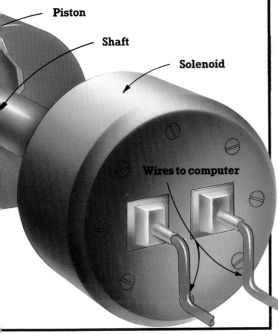

Piston

Shaft

Solenoid

Wires to computer

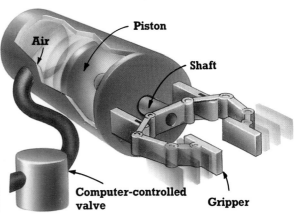

Piston

Air

Shaft

Computer-controlled valve

Gripper

## How to make your own pneumatic gripper

**You will need:** an empty detergent bottle, margarine tub, balloon, two pencils, cardboard, tape, two fine nails, hammer, sharp knife, scissors, sticky tape.

**1.** Carefully hammer nails through pencils half way along. Wiggle them around to make them loose. Cut two squares of cardboard as shown.

**2.** Cut holes in front and lid of tub in the places shown here, with sharp knife.

**3.** Tape cardboard to ends of pencils and push pencils through holes in the front of tub. Make sure nails are vertical and tape them to front of tub.

**4.** Remove cap of detergent bottle and put balloon on top. Push through hole in lid and between pencils. Squeeze bottle to inflate balloon and move "jaws". Try to seal the area between the detergent bottle and the tub with sticky tape.

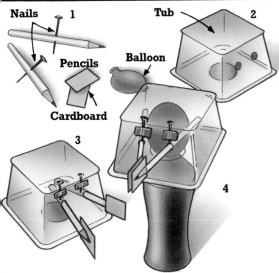

Nails  1

Tub  2

Pencils  Balloon

Cardboard

3

4

25

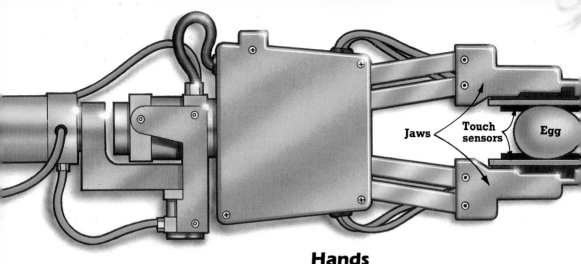

Jaws

Touch sensors

Egg

# How robots hold things

Before robots can do any work they need to be fitted with a tool or gripper – these items are known as end effectors. There are many different kinds of grippers and tools and they are often specially designed to do a particular job. These pages explain what some of them are and how they work.

## Hands

Some robots, like the one above, have grippers with jaws for grasping things. They have to be able to hold an object without either crushing it or letting it slip. This is difficult to control; the pressure must be just right, otherwise the robot may fling the object out of its grasp when it moves quickly. The jaws in the picture above have been fitted with touch, or tactile sensors, which tell the computer how tightly they are gripping. These enable the robot to apply the right amount of pressure to hold the object. The gripper "fingers" are specially shaped to keep the item in position.

## How robots change tools

A robot may need different tools to do a number of jobs and its computer can be programmed to make it change them automatically. The robot below holds tools with a bayonet fitting, like a light-bulb holder, attached to its wrist. The robot lowers the tool to be changed into a cradle, which holds it while the robot twists its wrist and pulls its arm away. The whole process is reversed to pick up another tool for the next stage in a job.

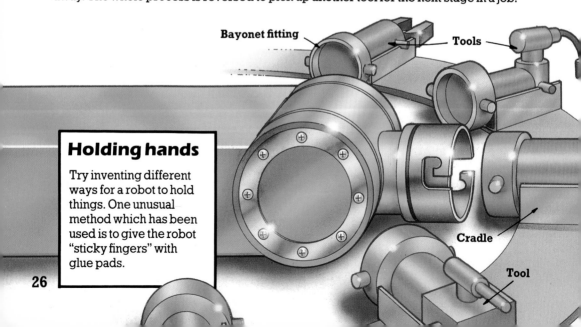

Bayonet fitting

Tools

### Holding hands

Try inventing different ways for a robot to hold things. One unusual method which has been used is to give the robot "sticky fingers" with glue pads.

Cradle

Tool

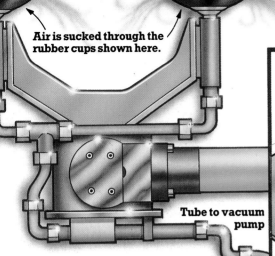

Air is sucked through the rubber cups shown here.

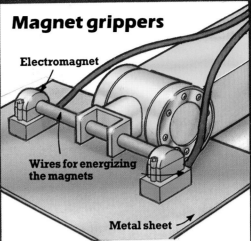

## Magnet grippers

Electromagnet

Wires for energizing the magnets

Metal sheet

Tube to vacuum pump

## Vacuum grippers

Vacuum grippers, like the ones above, are often used to pick up fragile objects – glass, or paper sacks, for example. The grippers are rubber cups and air is sucked through them in much the same way as a vacuum cleaner. This makes the object stick to the gripper. The flow of air is controlled by the computer and the weight the grippers are able to lift depends on how powerful the suction is.

## Holding tools

Many kinds of tools can be bolted directly to the robot's wrist. The robot below, for example, has a small electric grinder fixed to its wrist to take rough edges off pieces of metal. This method of holding a tool is used where the robot has to do the same job over and over again without the need for a tool change.

Electromagnets (electric magnets) are sometimes used as grippers for picking up metal objects. They are connected to a supply of electricity but are magnetic only when the power is switched on by the robot's computer. When there is no power, they usually lose their magnetism and drop things. Occasionally, objects need to be demagnetized.

## Make your own electromagnet

You can find out how an electromagnet works by making one with a large steel nail, a length of plastic-covered wire and a battery.

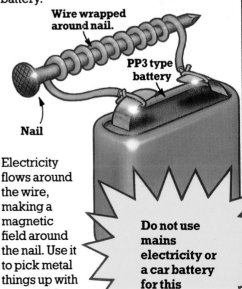

Wire wrapped around nail.

PP3 type battery

Nail

Electricity flows around the wire, making a magnetic field around the nail. Use it to pick metal things up with the tip of the nail.

Do not use mains electricity or a car battery for this experiment.

Electric grinder

Power lead

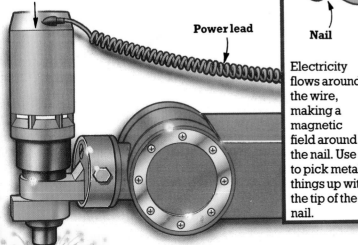

# Computer control

Computers are programmed to control robots by sending them instructions, which take the form of electrical signals. Computers can also be programmed to react to information from the robot's sensors. These pages explain how a robot arm's computer instructs it to assemble things on a conveyor belt. It also shows how messages from a TV camera sensor make the computer interrupt its instructions to the robot when something goes wrong on the conveyor – when a sleeping cat comes along, for example. All robots are computer-controlled and what they can do depends upon the program used.

## Computer messages

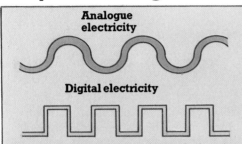

Analogue electricity

Digital electricity

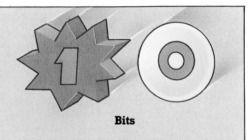

Bits

Most robots use electrical signals that rise and fall in strength like a continuous wave. This is called "analogue" electricity. Computer information is in a different form. The electrical signals are on or off, without any in-between stages, and the wave can be shown as a square pattern. This is called "digital".

Computers work using individual pulses of electricity called bits. There are two kinds – "no pulse" bits, written as 0, which have a very low electric current, and "pulse" bits, written as 1, which have a high current. This digital information uses the high (1) and low (0) signals as a counting system called binary.

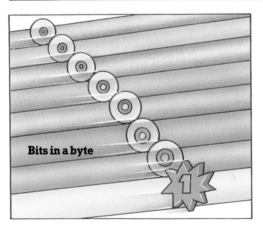

Bits in a byte

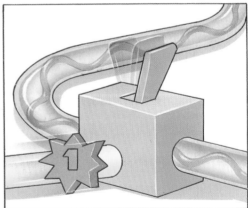

The computer is connected to the robot by eight or more wires called the bus. Many computers use groups of eight bits, called bytes, to represent pieces of information*. Each byte is an eight-digit code made up by 0s and 1s. Bytes of information from the computer to the motors, and the sensors to the computer, take turns to go along the same bus in opposite directions. This picture shows the eight bits of a byte travelling parallel to each other along a bus.

The digital instructions sent out by the computer go to an interface which has an electronic switch for each of the robot's motors. This picture shows what happens at one switch. The "pulse" bit in the byte turns the switch for one motor either on or off and allows the motor to rotate a fraction of a turn at each pulse. An interface is necessary because the motors do not work directly with digital pulses.

*Some computers have 32 bits.

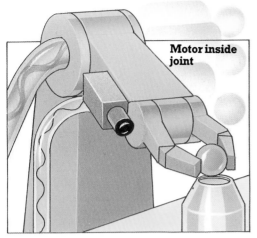

The analogue electricity powers a motor in one of the robot's joints – here it makes the arm go down to assemble two things on the conveyor.

The TV camera sensor on the side of the robot arm sends pictures of the scene on the conveyor to the computer. These are sent in the form of analogue electricity.

The analogue information from the TV camera is converted into digital information so that the computer can understand it. This is done by an interface, often called an analogue to digital converter.

The computer is programmed to analyse the information from the camera sensor and to react by stopping the robot if it cannot identify an object on the conveyor, such as a sleeping cat. The robot also stops if a part appears to be missing.

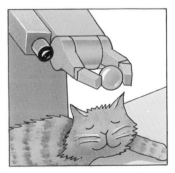

The computer sends out a byte with a "pulse" bit to the motor-switching interface, just as it did to turn the motor on.

The "pulse" bit switches off the analogue electricity flowing through the switch. The motor stops because it has no power.

The whole process of stopping the arm takes less than one hundredth of the time it would take you to blink. The cat is unharmed.

# Sensors

A robot's computer cannot know what is happening to the robot, or whether the robot has obeyed its instructions, unless it is equipped with sensors. There are two main types – those the robot uses to "touch" with, called contact sensors, and those used to "see" or "hear" with, called non-contact sensors.

Sensors work by sending an electric signal to the computer. The amount of electrical information the sensor sends out, called its output, depends on what the robot's environment does to it. A microphone "ear" would send a lot of information to the computer if someone standing next to the robot screamed, for example. Generally, the more that happens to the sensor, the greater its output.

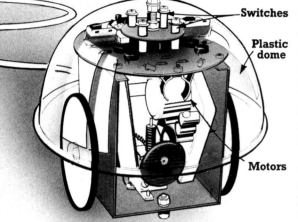

Switches

Plastic dome

Motors

## Hebot robot

The micro-robot on the left is equipped with the simplest kind of contact sensor – switches. There are four switches under the top of the plastic dome, which is loose. When the robot collides with something, the dome touches one of the switches, which sends a signal to the computer to reverse the robot's motors.

The robot can be programmed to move around like the Turtle and can also be equipped with a pen to draw pictures. The pen can be lifted up and down under the control of the computer.

## Touch sensors

Touch, or tactile sensors tell the computer when the robot is touching something. These sensors are often used on grippers and on the bumpers, or fenders, of mobile robots. The computer needs feedback from these sensors so that it can prevent the robot from crushing anything that it touches.

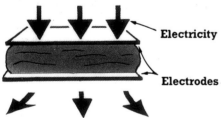

Electricity

Electrodes

The picture above shows a tactile sensor. It is made from a sandwich of special foam rubber between two pieces of metal that conduct electricity, called electrodes. When nothing is touching the electrodes, the foam in the middle stops electricity running from one to the other. If the sandwich is squeezed, some of the electricity gets through. By measuring this amount, the computer can tell how much pressure there is on the sensor.

A light load on the sensor allows a small amount of current to pass from one electrode to the other.

A heavy load squeezes the sensor more and lets a lot of electricity pass across the electrodes.

## Another touch sensor

This tactile sensor works by using two optical fibres inside a cylinder. Optical fibres are thin tubes of glass used to transmit light. The cylinder has a flexible mirror at one end and two holes in the other. A lamp shines a beam of light down one fibre onto the mirror, which reflects it up the other fibre, and into a photoelectric cell. This detects the amount of reflected light. When the flexible mirror is pressed, less light is reflected into the photoelectric cell. The computer can convert the amount of reflected light into a measurement of pressure on the mirror.

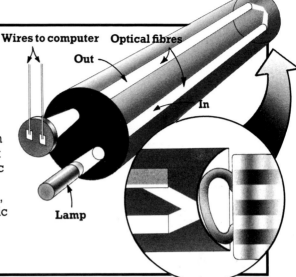

Wires to computer  Optical fibres

Out

In

Lamp

## Vision

One of the most powerful non-contact sensors is vision. The picture on the right shows a kind of camera, called a solid-state camera, connected to a computer. On the computer screen is the camera's view of a face.

The camera "views" an object with a grid of small, square, light-sensitive cells, each of which corresponds to a square on the screen. Each cell is electrically charged. Light areas of an object viewed with the camera make the cells lose a lot of their charge, while dark areas only make them lose a little. The computer converts the amount of charge on each cell into a square of light on the screen. This is called the "grey scale".

**Solid-state cameras often have over 400,000 cells within a single picture.**

Camera

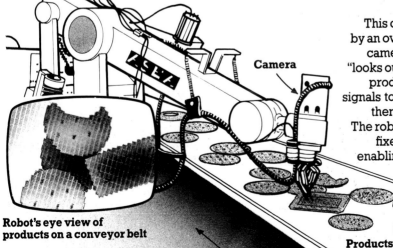

Camera

This conveyor is scanned by an overhead, wide-angle camera (not shown). This "looks out" for any imperfect products and then sends signals to the robot to remove them from the conveyor. The robot also has a camera fixed above its gripper, enabling it to "see" the sub-standard products.

**Robot's eye view of products on a conveyor belt**

Products

Direction of conveyor

# How a robot knows where it is

Two different kinds of sensor enable a robot's computer to know where the robot is. Proximity sensors measure the distance between a robot and an object. Positional sensors tell the computer by how much part of a robot has moved.

## How a mobile robot knows where it is

A mobile robot has to be equipped with both types of sensor. It can then avoid collisions by measuring distances, and can follow a programmed path by calculating its position. One way of doing this is with an ultrasonic sensor, shown below on an experimental tractor. "Bleeps" of sound are transmitted that bounce back from surrounding objects. The computer works out where the robot is from the delay between sending the sound and hearing its echo, called a "time of flight" recording. This is the same method bats use to fly in the dark.

### Puzzle

Sound travels about 330 metres (about 360 yards) in one second. It takes 1½ seconds for the sound to go from this robot's sensor to the tree and back again. How far away is the tree from the robot?

**This "bleep" is too high for humans to hear. The robot may generate more than 1000 bleeps in less than a second.**

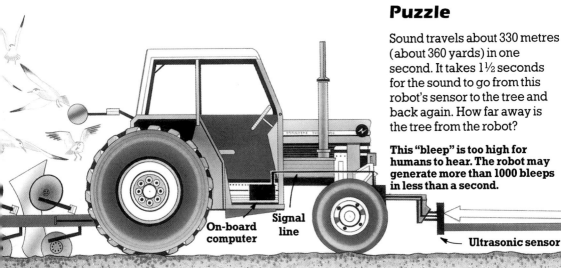

On-board computer

Signal line

Ultrasonic sensor

## How robots measure bends

Coded disc

Wire to computer

Reading head

Wire to computer

A robot arm's computer needs to know that the robot has carried out its instructions by finding out the position of the arm. This robot has a sensor called an optical position encoder on each of its joints which measures how much it has bent its arm and wrist. Each sensor sends a digital message to the computer which it converts into an angular measurement. The sensor has two parts – a flat disc with marks on it, and a reading head which "reads" the marks. Each segment on the disc represents a number in binary code. The disc is attached to a part of the robot which moves, and the reading head is fixed to a part which stays still. As the arm bends a different black and white pattern is "read" from the disc and this number is sent to the computer.

# How a robot arm knows where it is

Sensors can be fixed to a robot arm to give its computer arm-movement measurements. Some sensors are used to make straight-line measurements, and others to measure angles.

One way of making measurements is with a sensor called an electrical potentiometer. This works like a dimmer switch by varying the amount of electricity passing along a wire. The amount of electricity getting through the wire can be converted into a measurement by connecting it via an interface to the computer.

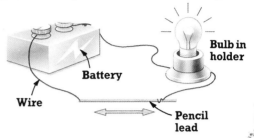

**Bulb in holder**

**Battery**

**Wire**

**Pencil lead**

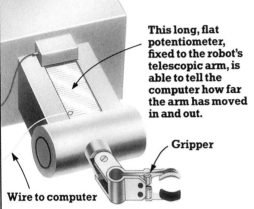

This long, flat potentiometer, fixed to the robot's telescopic arm, is able to tell the computer how far the arm has moved in and out.

**Gripper**

**Wire to computer**

▲
You can test the principle of a potentiometer using a battery\*, wire, lamp and a pencil. Carefully split the pencil down the middle, take the lead out and connect everything together as shown. By sliding one end of the wire up and down the pencil lead, you can vary the brightness of the bulb. This happens because the lead resists the flow of electricity.

A special kind of wire which does the same thing as the pencil lead in the experiment shown above, is used in a potentiometer.

---

The first segment has 3 white parts (000), and the eighth segment has 3 black parts (111).

**Bits to computer**

0    0    1

**Photodetector**

**Black part**

**...led disc**

**Lamp**

**Shiny part**

**Fifth segment**

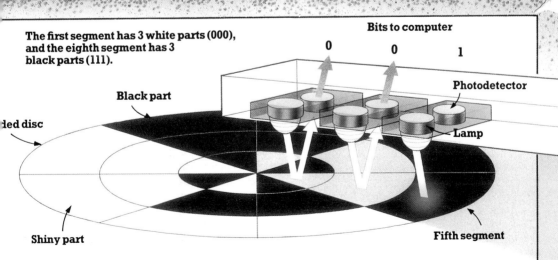

Shiny white parts of the disc, which reflect the light into the photodetectors, are registered as 0's. Black parts, which absorb the light, are registered as 1's.

The fifth segment is shown under the reading head and has the binary pattern 001. This is called a 3-bit code because the sensor sends three bits to the computer.

*\*DO NOT use mains electricity for this experiment. This would be very dangerous.*

# Cybernetics

Cybernetics is the science of control and communication in both machines and living organisms. The word comes from a Greek word meaning "steersman". It is particularly the study of self-controlling, or adaptive, systems. These alter behaviour because of changes in environment. For example, the automatic pilot used in aircraft alters the course of the plane as a result of changes in the wind speed.

## Artificial intelligence

Artificial intelligence (AI) is a field that is closely related to cybernetics. It is about making machines do intelligent things. Machines have to be able to "think" to do something intelligent, but experts disagree about what this means. Some machines, called Knowledge-Based Systems (KBS), are able to "learn" from past experience, or respond to things happening to them. Some people believe that these machines can be called "thinking" machines. Others argue that for machines to think they must have feelings and want to do things. This would mean that a "thinking" robot, for instance, would have to want to pack boxes because it enjoyed its work.

## Clever machines

Computers are the cleverest machines available. By ingenious programming and technology they can be made to simulate, or mimic, intelligent human activity, such as the processing of visual information and the creation of speech. Computers can be used to control other machines, such as robots, and make them behave "intelligently".

## "Intelligent" computer

Computers use programs in two basic ways. Algorithmic programs, often used for robots, use the coded information from sensors to make decisions by a process of elimination. Highly efficient heuristic programs take short-cuts to the best solutions by comparing feedback with information stored in a Knowledge Base. A robot computer could play chess using either a program of the game's rules, or by comparing the state of play against a memory store of all the possible moves.

## Speech recognition

Computer programs are being developed to give robots the ability to recognize spoken commands, using a microphone as an electronic "ear". The average adult knows thousands of words, so it would take a computer with a massive memory to understand even a tiny fraction of them. The computer also has to take into account the different ways that people speak. It is much simpler to program the computer to recognize only a short list of words, spoken by one person, which are needed for the robot's job.

## How computers recognize words

**1.** Each word makes a unique pattern of signals that are received by a microphone and then converted into electricity. The waves vary according to the different sounds in a word. The diagram below shows what the word "faster" would look like to a computer.

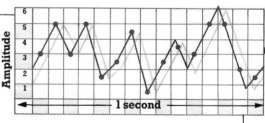

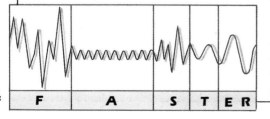

**2.** The height of the wave, called the amplitude, shows an electrical voltage that is measured many times a second. This series of measurements is turned into a code of "pulse" and "no pulse" bits which the computer then uses to identify the word. The pattern above shows the first two bytes of the word "faster" in one second.

# Vision

More and more robots have machine vision, which allows them to "see" and behave "intelligently". However, humans are selective in what they see, whereas a computer can only "see" the images it is instructed and programmed to recognize. For example, if you look carefully at this picture you can choose to see either a vase or two faces. A computer vision system would need instructions to "see" either a white image or a black image. It could only recognize this image by looking for a match with patterns stored in its memory and using the name given to the pattern in the program.

## How robots recognize things

A machine vision system can be programmed to recognize one or more views of the same object. This shows how an object in a pile can be recognized by a vision system so a robot can pick it up correctly for packing in a box.

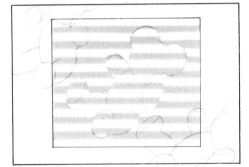

The system focuses on one part of the pile and projects a pattern of light over it to judge how far away it is. This information is sent to the robot's computer.

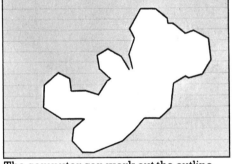

The computer can work out the outline of one bear from the breaks in the pattern of light. It is programmed only to identify the outlines of bears and will not recognize anything else.

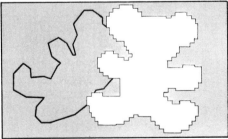

By comparing this outline with views of the bear stored in its memory, the computer can work out the position of the bear in the pile. The matching of outlines of an object in different positions is called "transformation".

The information is sent to the robot in the form of instructions to its motors. The computer controls the robot to pick the bear up without damaging it or any of the other bears. It then turns it the right way round for packing.

# Versatile robots

Robotics is a fast-moving and exciting subject with many research projects going on around the world. More and more robot arms are being used in factories along with other automatic machines. Robots are also becoming increasingly "intelligent", with more sophisticated sensors being developed all the time, together with clever computer programs. This means that mobile and other kinds of robots may soon become more familiar – perhaps in the home as robot "servants", or cleaning railway stations or hospitals at night when few people are around to obstruct them.

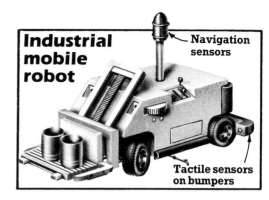

**Industrial mobile robot**

Navigation sensors

Tactile sensors on bumpers

This is a driverless forklift truck which will be used in an automated warehouse or factory. It has an on-board computer and power supply and uses sensors to navigate.

## Nuclear reactor robot

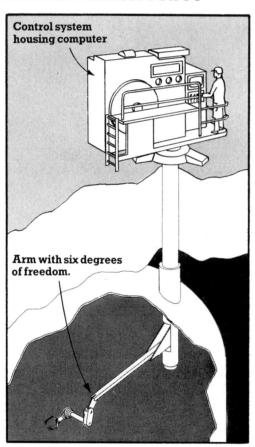

Control system housing computer

Arm with six degrees of freedom.

This robot arm is designed to be used in the core of a nuclear reactor. The arm is suspended from a long hollow tube. Control cables for the arm pass through the tube with safety seals to ensure that no radiation leaks can occur.

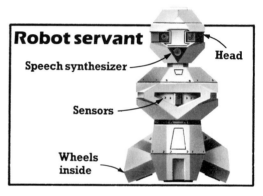

**Robot servant**

Head

Speech synthesizer

Sensors

Wheels inside

This robot can be programmed to do things like serve drinks at a party and speak to guests with its synthesized voice. Others are being made which do housework.

**Robot trains**

Completely automatic robot trains are used on the Paris Metro in France and on the Dockland's Light Railway in London. The trains are computer-controlled to switch between tracks and are programmed to stop at stations.

## Robot computer assistant

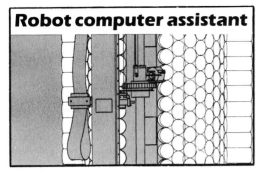

This robot arm goes up and down in a honeycomb storage cell to find special cartridges containing computer tapes. It delivers the cartridges to the computer and replaces them after use.

## Two-armed robot

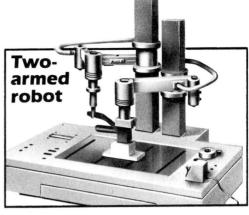

Yes-Man is a special robot designed to work alongside humans on a production line. Its arms allow it to do complex assembly work – it can even do two things at once. The base contains control microcomputers.

## Walking robot

Scientists in Japan, the US and Europe have built four-legged walking robots that can climb stairs and carry large loads over uneven surfaces. Researchers are also trying out six- and eight-legged designs which walk like insects.

## Modular arm robot

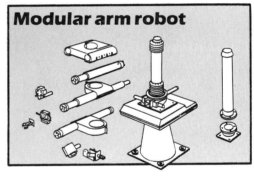

Some robot arms are being made in modules – small units, such as arm, wrist, base and so on – that can be combined in different ways to make a robot suitable for a particular job. They can be mounted on the floor, the wall or the ceiling.

## Robot cleaning machine

Twin scrubbing brushes

Free-roving, industrial floor-scrubbing robots are being developed. Together with navigation sensors, each will have a "map" of the building stored in the computer memory. Sensors will detect when the water becomes dirty and needs changing.

## Snooker-playing robot

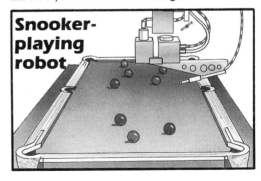

This robot arm plays a game of snooker, using a self-activating cue. A vision system uses two cameras to identify the positions and colours of the balls on the table. The computer is programmed to decide which are the best shots to play.

# Robots for dangerous work

Engineers have produced robots which are able to take the place of humans doing dangerous work. In some hazardous environments, such as in nuclear plants, humans can only work for short periods at a time. There are other situations where it is too dangerous for humans to work at all, such as in very deep seas. Specially designed robots can work quickly and safely in such unhealthy or dangerous situations and can be easily repaired or replaced if damaged.

## Imitating humans

Although it is still too difficult to create robots that behave as humans, some are now being made which imitate the workings of the human body. These robots are used in safety tests and other dangerous research, to avoid any risk to human life.

The US army uses a robot called LIFEMAN to learn more about the injuries that might occur to people manning military equipment while fighting. LIFEMAN has a fully-moveable skeleton, and can be put in any human position.

There are tiny electronic sensors in its head, back and legs to measure movement. Its chest is made of protective layers of fibre sheets, which, with the robot's life-like plastic skin, can be used to measure the force of any fragments which may hit it.

The robot shown on the left has been developed to test the protective clothing worn by people who work in dangerous environments, such as those with dangerous chemicals and extremes of temperature.

The robot is called MANNY and is very similar to the human body in size and moveability. MANNY's skeleton is covered with a flexible skin and has 12 heaters which alter its "body temperature". The robot is so life-like it even sweats, by injecting water through a network of narrow tubes. It can change the rate at which it sweats depending on its rate of exercise. It also imitates breathing by means of an artificial mouth and nose. MANNY's activities are controlled in a nearby room, where the wear and tear on the clothes is also monitored.

## Robot firemen

By the end of the 1990s fire-fighting robots may be a common sight. Researchers in Japan are developing a robot which has 6 leg-wheels to enable it to move quickly and overcome obstacles. It will "see" through smoke by using a laser and ultrasound, and two arms will operate a manipulator and a hose. The robot will also "sweat" by spraying fine jets of water, to keep its electronics cool in the intense heat.

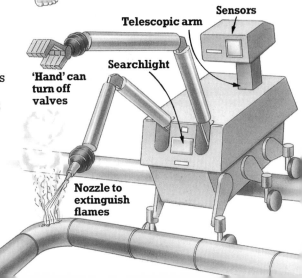

Sensors

Telescopic arm

Searchlight

'Hand' can turn off valves

Nozzle to extinguish flames

## Remotely-controlled robots

"Telechiric devices" are robots that are controlled at a distance by humans. These combine the best features of both people and robots. A robot can be programmed to carry out a sequence of operations more efficiently than a human worker. However, unlike most robots, humans are able to adapt their working patterns quickly to cope with unexpected changes in their environment. Telechiric devices are of most use in dangerous conditions where people might get hurt.

## Investigating suspicious objects

Bomb-disposal robot vehicles are telechiric devices that are now used all over the world for dealing with unexploded bombs. Explosives left in public places by terrorists are often booby-trapped, with trip wires to set them off. Before the invention of unmanned robot vehicles, disposing of these unexploded devices was a dangerous job that had to be carried out by hand.

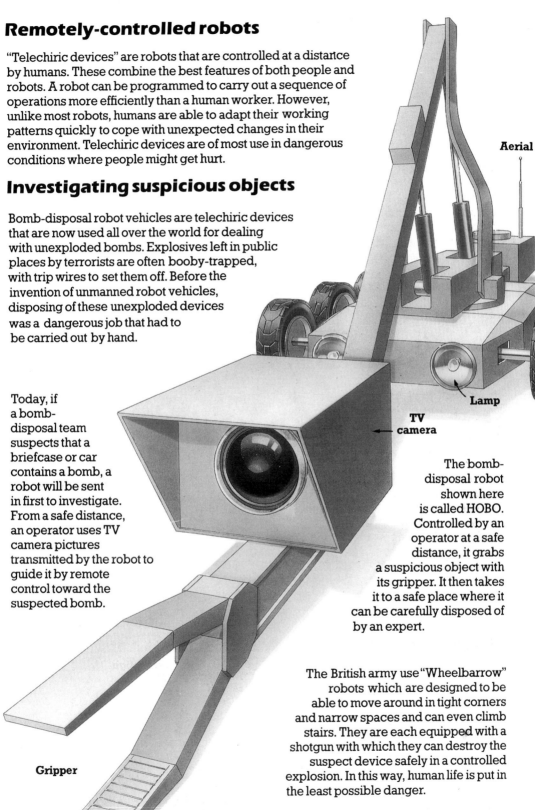

**Aerial**

**Lamp**

**TV ◄ camera**

**Gripper**

Today, if a bomb-disposal team suspects that a briefcase or car contains a bomb, a robot will be sent in first to investigate. From a safe distance, an operator uses TV camera pictures transmitted by the robot to guide it by remote control toward the suspected bomb.

The bomb-disposal robot shown here is called HOBO. Controlled by an operator at a safe distance, it grabs a suspicious object with its gripper. It then takes it to a safe place where it can be carefully disposed of by an expert.

The British army use "Wheelbarrow" robots which are designed to be able to move around in tight corners and narrow spaces and can even climb stairs. They are each equipped with a shotgun with which they can destroy the suspect device safely in a controlled explosion. In this way, human life is put in the least possible danger.

39

# Research projects

Engineers are trying to find ways in which robots can be used outside factories, in everyday life. Sensors can give advanced robots enough feedback to operate in unknown and unadapted environments. New technology has also enabled some robot computers to decide on certain actions for themselves.

## Robot builders

A wall-climbing robot has been designed for the building industry. It carries equipment on its back to clean, paint or repair buildings. It is controlled from ground level via a cable and can move over ceilings or walls while gripping the surface with suction pads. It also has its own built-in sensors. The largest of these robots can carry 70 kilograms (154 lbs) of equipment for cutting and welding.

## Walking machine

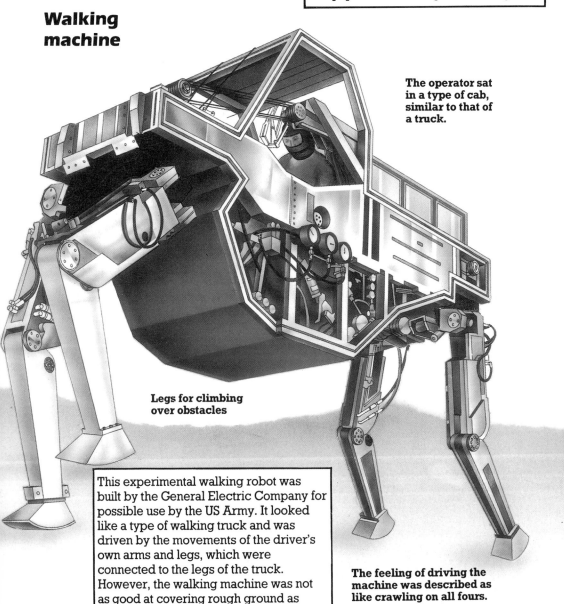

The operator sat in a type of cab, similar to that of a truck.

Legs for climbing over obstacles

This experimental walking robot was built by the General Electric Company for possible use by the US Army. It looked like a type of walking truck and was driven by the movements of the driver's own arms and legs, which were connected to the legs of the truck. However, the walking machine was not as good at covering rough ground as vehicles with tracks.

The feeling of driving the machine was described as like crawling on all fours.

## Finding a route

A computer program that will help industrial robots to move around in factories and cluttered conditions has been designed in America. A new technique gives a robot the ability to automatically reverse out of dead ends, to avoid obstructions, and turn itself around into the right positions, as shown in the picture. Its computer can solve any problems it encounters in a fraction of a second.

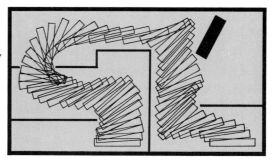

## Improving robot vision

The most exciting advances in robotics may come from providing robots with improved means of sight. Researchers in America have solved a major problem in enabling robots to "see" like humans. When a subject moves towards you, each eye adjusts itself to keep the subject in focus. This process is known as vergence. Advances in computer technology and the development of fast and accurate motor controllers have made this possible for robots. The controllers can swivel a robot's camera-eyes separately, and almost as fast as human eye movements, in order to focus. The camera images never overlap, so "cross-eyed" vision is avoided.

**Cross-eyed vision as the subject approaches.**

**A clear focus on the moving subject.**

## Virtual reality

American and British scientists have developed special equipment which enables computer operators to sense and control the world of computer graphics, called "cyberspace". This new type of experience and manipulation is called virtual reality. The Teletact glove allows a computer operator to "touch" objects produced on a computer as if they were 3-dimensional solids. The DataGlove is able to transmit the wearer's hand movements into the computer. This technique will save time and money when designing industrial robots, as both the machine and its workspace can be fully explored while they are still only images on a computer screen.

By using virtual reality, robots which replace humans in dangerous situations will be able to relay information about their environment back to an operator through not only visual, but also tactile and audio means. Engineers at the National Advanced Robotics Research Centre (UK) are working on this type of robot for VERDEX – the Virtual Environment Remote Driving Experiment. A robot is remotely-controlled by an operator wearing a special headset. This shows both the robot's camera image of the road ahead, and computer-generated driving controls. The aim is true "telepresence" – where the operator feels that they are actually there.

# Latest developments

## Robots in industry

A completely automated factory is a goal that many engineers have been working towards for years. Some energy would be saved as the factory would not need to be lit or heated for human workers. Space would not be wasted by safety considerations and noise levels would not be a problem. A demonstration factory was set-up in Tokyo in 1990 where different machines in offices, design studios and production areas communicated through several computer languages. This was the first time it had been proved possible to run an entire business, from head office to design studio to shop floor, on a network of computers and robots.

## Robots which help human mobility

Exoskeletons are robots that fit around a human body and help to increase muscle strength. Although the machines are awkward and unattractive, they do help people with disabilities that affect their arm and leg movements. Unfortunately, exoskeletons can only help people with some existing movement.

Much progress has been made in using robotics to control artificial limbs. Messages from the brain are sent to the artificial limb via electrical contacts, called actuators. These link the artificial limb directly to the nervous system. An artificial arm or leg will then work in the same way as a natural one, although with less freedom of movement.

## Destructive robots

Modern flying weapons, such as cruise missiles, are robot weapons controlled by computers. Their control systems use electronic maps and information received from space satellites to keep them flying on course. They also use radar sensors to pick up anything in their path, enabling them to steer around obstacles.

## Robot help in the home

Robots are being tested that can fetch and carry, to help people with disabilities in their own homes. Guided by wires fitted under the carpet, the robot would be able to move around safely. It would be programmed to recognize objects, so that it could find a pizza in the fridge, and cook it in the microwave, for example. A special arm might also be attached for reaching and holding objects and, if necessary, to help the operator to feed themself. The robot could be controlled by speech, whistling, or via a keyboard, depending on the abilities of the operator.

## Filling station robot attendant

The Swedish "Tankomatic" robot allows people to fill up the fuel tanks of their cars without getting out of the vehicle. Cars with specially adapted fuel caps park next to the machine and insert a credit card. Guided by sensors, the robot finds and opens the cap and puts its nozzle into the tank. When the robot has filled the tank with fuel it automatically withdraws and locks the cap, allowing the driver to drive off.

## Robots on the farm

A cow-milking robot has been developed which works without the farmer being present. When a cow enters an empty milking-stall, a radio transmitter in the stall sends a signal to a receiver around the cow's neck. This identifies the cow, and a computer checks data in its memory to see if it is due for milking. Ultrasound beams are used to find the udder and teats, then the robot arm carefully attaches the milking system. As the cows are free to present themselves for milking as often as they like, milk production is increased.

## Robots for cleaning aircraft

A computerised robot arm with a reach of 26 metres has been designed and tested as a cleaning system for aircraft. The arm has eight joints, more than most industrial robots, and has a rotating brush on the end. The control system allows the arm either to be programmed, or operated manually with a joystick. However, the huge size and weight of the arm makes it quite difficult to position the cleaning head accurately. Even so, it usually takes 12 people eight hours to clean a jumbo jet, but the robot arm did the job in only three.

## Automatic digger

A robot excavator has been developed in the U.K. that digs without the need for a human operator. After it has been driven into position, the excavator is guided by a laser beam, with an on-board computer to control the bucket and work out the best way to dig. The robot is even more accurate than a skilled human operator. Safety is also improved. When used in dangerous conditions, such as digging up leaking gas pipes, the excavator can be operated by using a remote-control.

## Robotic surgery

A robot precision drill is now being used during ear operations to help restore hearing. A surgeon guides the positioning of the drill, but the drilling itself is carried out automatically. The robot tool is more accurate than a human in drilling the tiny bone in the middle ear. The same technology is being adapted for other parts of the body, and has already been used in over 500 brain operations.

## Robot butcher

Researchers have produced a robot that can carve up a beef carcass. The robot feels its way along the bones of a carcass, removing the meat with a twin-blade knife. Sensors monitor the shape of the bone inside the carcass and guide the robot's 'hand'.

## Robot chef

Just as they already assemble many of the world's cars, robots may soon make many of the world's hamburgers. Engineers at a major fast-food company have been developing equipment to automatically carry out all food preparation and cooking by a robot. Staff will be left to take orders and enter this information into a computer. The robot will then cook and deliver as much food as the computer thinks the customers will need. The system is now ready to use, although it is still cheaper to employ people than install the multi-talented robot.

## Hospital helpers

An advanced mobile robot is in service in American hospitals. It has been designed to save the time of doctors and nurses by transporting materials and equipment from one part of a hospital to another. The robot does not need an especially adapted environment. It performs errands without needing a track and guides itself by means of vision and ultrasonic proximity sensors. It plans the best route by using a map of the building stored in its computer memory. A large screen enables the operator to give the robot instructions once it has reached its destination. The robot can even use elevators on its own.

Research is being carried out into other ways in which robots might be of help with tasks that are tiring for medical staff. A robot called PAM (the Patient Assistant for Mobility) has been produced in the U.K. It is hoped that this will solve the problem of lifting patients and moving them from one position to another. Arms, similar to those on a fork-lift truck, slide under the patient and transfer them onto the trolley-like robot. A nurse operates the robot by remote control and can program it with information about the patient's shape and injury, so that they are lifted with care.

# Robot words

The following glossary gives explanations of many of the terms used in this book as well as some new ones:

**Actuator:** An actuator responds to computer signals by producing hydraulic, electrical or pneumatic energy. This energy is used to drive the robot's moving parts.

**Advanced robot:** A robot that uses sensors and machine intelligence to plan its own actions and to monitor and react to changes in the environment.

**Android:** A robot that is made to look and act like a human. Androids are more common in films, science fiction and exhibitions than in day-to-day life.

**Artificial Intelligence (AI):** The study of making machines do "intelligent things". Experts disagree on a precise definition as to what counts as intelligence or intelligent behaviour.

**Automated Guided Vehicle (AGV):** A driverless truck that moves around a factory area by either remote control or via an internal computer program.

**Automation:** The use of automatic machines without direct human control.

**Binary System:** A system of numbers used in computing. Only the digits 0 and 1 are used.

**Computer:** A machine that uses small electrical currents flowing through circuits to make rapid calculations, to store and analyse information, or to control machinery automatically.

**Computer-Aided Design (CAD):** The use of computers to assist in the creation of designs.

**Computer-Aided Manufacturing (CAM):** The use of computers in all stages of production.

**Control box:** The part of a robot that tells it what to do, usually the computer.

**Cybernetics:** The science of control and communication in both machines and living organisms.

**Data processing:** The conversion of information, usually by a computer, into material that can be used to solve problems or to produce further information.

**Degrees of freedom:** A technical term used to describe the number of different directions in which a robot arm can move. Usually the more joints a robot has in its arm, the more degrees of freedom it has.

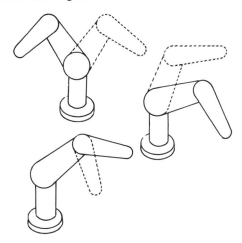

**Electronic device:** A piece of electrical equipment containing transistors and other electronic circuit components.

**End effector:** The name given to all types of tooling attached to the active end of a robot, e.g. a gripper.

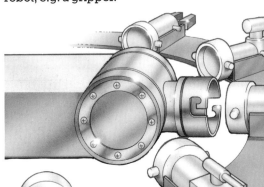

**Feedback:** Information about the robot or its surroundings that a computer gets from sensors on the robot.

**First generation robots:** Robots without sensors of any kind. They are controlled by a fixed sequence of instructions stored in the computer programme or control box.

**Flexible automation:** Describes the adaptability of robots, which are capable of being reprogrammed to perform many tasks.

**Gantry:** An overhead framework, often used for supporting robots.

**Generation:** This is the term used to describe the groups into which robots are classified.

**Gears:** These reduce or increase the speed of a motor. They are used between a motor and the part of a robot that it drives.

**Gripper:** The mechanism fixed to a robot arm's wrist to hold things. Sometimes called an end effector.

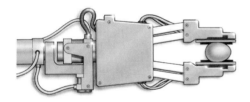

**Hydraulic system:** A device using special oil in pipes and cylinders to drive the mechanical part of a robot. Often used in robot arms which need greater strength for heavy work.

**Knowledge Based System (KBS):** A system that uses a set of "rules" from past experience to determine the current course of action for the robot to take.

**Lead-through programming:** A way of teaching a robot by guiding it through the movements needed to do a job.

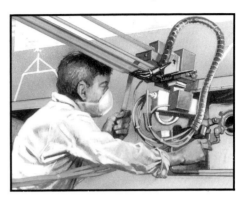

**LOGO:** A computer language often used to program robots which draw, such as the Turtle.

**Machine vision:** A computer-controlled device used to give robots a primitive kind of sight.

**Manipulator:** Robot arms can also be called manipulators.

**Memory:** Where programs and data are stored in a computer.

**Microcomputer:** These store vast quantities of data on single chips of silicon, and are smaller and cheaper than mainframe computers.

**Navigation:** How a computer uses information from a mobile robot's sensors to get the robot from one place to another without bumping into anything. **45**

**Odometer:** A sensor that measures the distance travelled by a wheeled vehicle.

**Optosensor:** A sensor that uses light as its sensing medium.

**Photoelectric cell:** An electronic device which detects light. These are often used as part of a sensor on robots.

**Pitch:** The name for the up and down movement in a robot's wrist, like the movement made when shaking hands.

**Pneumatic system:** A device powered by air or another gas to operate a mechanical part of a robot – often the gripper.

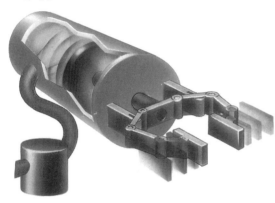

**Port:** The socket on a computer where interfaces and other kinds of electronic equipment are plugged in.

**Program:** A sequence of instructions given to a computer that controls everything the robot does.

**Robot:** A computer-controlled machine which can be programmed to do different kinds of things. Experts do not agree on an exact definition of a robot.

**Robotics:** The study of robots and the associated automation technology. Originated by Isaac Asimov.

**Roll:** A name for the movement in a robots's wrist which goes from side to side like rocking a boat.

**Second generation robots:** Robots with one or more sensors which may be used to alter the work sequence.

**Sensor:** A device which gives a robot's computer information either about the robot or its surroundings.

**Sonar sensor:** Often used for navigation, these sensors emit a sound and then "listen" for an echo to bounce back from obstacles. Distances are calculated from the time taken for the sound to return.

**Speech synthesizer:** An electronic device, often a chip, which can be programmed to produce words and sentences through a loudspeaker. Each word is broken down into small units of sound, which are then reproduced from a computer.

**Teleoperation:** When the robot is controlled remotely by an operator.

**Third generation robot:** A robot with artificial intelligence.

**Transformer:** An electrical device which converts mains electricity into lower level voltage suitable for use inside computers and other equipment.

**Turtle:** A wheeled micro-robot programmed to move about and draw, using a computer language called LOGO.

**Vision robot:** A robot equipped with a TV camera to enable it to "see" what it is doing.

**Working envelope:** The area of space that a robot arm is able to reach.

**Yaw:** The name given to the left and right movement in a robot's wrist – similar to the movement made steering a bicycle.

# Index

The publishers would like to thank the following for their help:

Koorosh Khodabandehloo, Bristol University
(snooker-playing robot and robot butcher).
Valiant Technology Ltd. (Turtle).
Armstrong Projects Ltd.
(PAM-Patient Assistant for Mobility).
LEGO U.K. Limited (Buggy).
Andrew Lennard, Colne Robotics Co. Ltd.
John Jessop, Jessop Microelectronics Ltd.
Peter Mathews, Upperdata Ltd.
Dr George Russell, Heriot-Watt University.
Milton Bradley Europe.
Economatics Ltd.